Gardner B. Perry

# History of Bradford, Mass.

Anatiposi

**Gardner B. Perry**

# History of Bradford, Mass.

Reprint of the original, first published in 1872.

1st Edition 2023  |  ISBN: 978-3-38212-844-9

Anatiposi Verlag is an imprint of Outlook Verlagsgesellschaft mbH.

Verlag (Publisher): Outlook Verlag GmbH, Zeilweg 44, 60439 Frankfurt, Deutschland
Vertretungsberechtigt (Authorized to represent): E. Roepke, Zeilweg 44, 60439 Frankfurt, Deutschland
Druck (Print): Books on Demand GmbH, In de Tarpen 42, 22848 Norderstedt, Deutschland

# HISTORY OF BRADFORD, MASS.,

FROM

## THE EARLIEST PERIOD

TO THE CLOSE OF 1820,

BY

## GARDNER B. PERRY, A. M.

(As contained in his Historical Sermon delivered Dec. 30, 1820.)

HAVERHILL, MASS:
C. C. MORSE & SON, BOOK AND JOB PRINTERS.
1872.

Most of the facts contained in this discourse have been gathered by personal enquiry.  It is not improbable there may be a trifling inaccuracy in some of the dates, though I can  hardly think  after all that has been done to get to the truth, there will be found many very important errors on this subject.  But as the memories of men are not always to be depended upon, it may be proper to observe, I  have  endeavored to state the truth, and believe I have taken proper  pains  to ascertain it.  With these observations, I now commit the discourse to my beloved people, for whose entertainment it was at first written, with my  best wishes for  their temporal  and spiritual welfare.                                                   THE AUTHOR.

# DISCOURSE.



## 2 KINGS XX. 20.

And the rest of the acts of Hezekiah, and all his might, and how he made a pool, and a conduit, and brought water into the city, are they not written in the book of the chronicles of the kings of Judah?

THE countenance afforded in this and many other passages of scripture, to the habit of recording what men do, and the improvements they make in the various business of life, will be my support in calling your attention this day to some of the events connected with the history of this town.

It is well known to you, that two hundred years have now rolled away, since the first settlement was made in Plymouth by a company of men, whose object, as expressed by themselves, was "to walk in all the ways of God made known or to be made known to them, according to their best endeavours." This prepared the way for others to come; and in the year 1628, the proprietors of that section of this country, which constitutes the greater part of this commonwealth, sent over Mr. Endicotte with about a hundred planters, who arrived at the place now called Salem, the 6th of September the same year, and laid the foundation of that town. The next summer, this new Colony received an accession of above three hundred planters more, and with them, two eminent divines, Mr. Francis Higginson and Samuel Skelton. Soon after their arrival, that is, on the 6th of August, the persons proposing to unite in church relation, gave their public assent to a confession of faith, and then solemnly convenanted with God and each other, to walk in the ordinances of Christ. Messrs. Higginson and Skelton were then set apart as ministers of said church, the former as teacher, the latter as pastor, at which solemnity the church at Plymouth assisted by their delegate. This was the first church fully organized in New England; that at Plymouth, the only one of an earlier date, had not a regular pastor till after this. On the 30th of July, 1636, Governor Winthrop, Lieutenant Governor Dudley, Mr. Johnson and Mr. Wilson, entered into a formal and solemn covenant of faith and practice, according to the gospel and laid the foundation of the first church in Charlestown, where on the 27th of August following, Mr. Wilson was ordained pastor, which was the first ordination in this state. In March, 1633, John Winthrop, son of the governor, with twelve men began a plantation at what is now called Ipswich, the next year a church was formed, and in April, the people being without a minister, the governor walked there on foot from Boston, spent the sabbath and exercised himself by way of *Prophesying*, that is in public teaching and exhortation. In 1634, Nathaniel Ward, from England, became their minister, and on the 20th of February, 1639, Mr. Nathaniel Rogers was settled in the same place as colleague with Mr. Norton, who succeeded Mr. Ward, and it was this last circumstance which led to the settlement of Rowley, of which this town formerly constituted a part; for when Mr. Ezekiel Rogers, with about sixty industrious families came from Yorkshire, in England, to this country, he was influenced in his choice of a place of settlement, by a desire of being near and enjoying the company of Nathaniel Rogers, who we have mentioned as settled in Ipswich. Mr. Rogers arrived in this country in the fall of 1628. He called the place of his settlement Rowley, after the place where he had formerly served in the gospel of Christ. As many of your ancestors sat under his ministry, you will feel a special interest in him when you attend to a short account of his life. He was a man of considerable note, as is evident from his preaching the election sermon in 1643, only about four years after his arrival. He was abundant in his labours, and for several of the first years of his ministry enjoyed much peace and comfort with his people, saw the work of God flourish and grow among them. But after the settlement of a colleague, which happened about ten or twelve years after his arrival in this country, and which seemed to be necessary from the numerous calls he had to attend to, there arose jealousies and contentions among his people, which rendered the remainder of his life unhappy. He experienced also domestic affliction, buried two wives, all his children, and had his house and most of his papers burned on the night following his third marriage. This last circumstance renders our information concerning the early history of this town less perfect than it would otherwise have been. He lost also the use of his right arm by a fall from his horse, and was obliged, late in life, to learn to write with his left hand. But he seems, through the grace of God, to have been generally patient and submissive under these manifold tribulations, and to adopt what I suppose was his own expression on the subject, ' to have believed and expected after having made the voyage of this life over a troubled sea, he should reach the haven of everlasting rest.' His last sickness was of a lingering nature, which he bore with christian patience, and died January 22, 1668, aged 79. He left his property, which was considerable, to the town of Rowley, for the support of the gospel. His will, which I have seen, is still in good preservation.*

Many of the inhabitants who came with Mr. Rogers, were weavers ; and soon after their arrival in this country they set up a fulling mill, employed their children in spin-

* A part of this property, in consequence of the towns not having complied with a condition contained in the Will, has fallen to Harvard College.

ning cotton, and were the first who manufactured cloth in North America.

Just at what time this part of the town was settled I have not been able to ascertain. It was not however long after the first settlement in Rowley, and as it appears by some of the younger families who came to that place. The first house built in the town, was on the north of the road leading to Haverhill, and about 40 rods above Mr. Francis Kimball's, where the cellar may yet be seen. It was owned by a Mr. Jackson, whose christian name was probably William.

The first meeting for town affairs on record, was held the 20th of February, 1668. The name then given to this town was Merrimack. It was afterwards called Rowley Village. At a meeting held January 7, 1672, the vote passed to call the town Bradford, and the town was incorporated by this name in 1673. But though as we have said the first meeting on record was in 1668, it does not appear that this was, by any means, tho first time the people on this river, met by themselves in town affairs, for at that time they had a meeting house erected and also a parsonage. Many circumstances render it probable that almost from the first settlement, though connected with Rowley, and acting with them in many common concerns, yet living at such a distance, they held town meetings, among themselves, chose their own officers, and managed all those concerns which did not interfere with the interest of the other settlement in town, according to their own discretion. And among the circumstances which renders this opinion plausible, is that Bradford and Boxford, though making but one town with Rowley, were not within the first patent granted to Mr. Rogers, but were the next year granted to him and to Mr. John Phillips, at the very earnest requestof Mr. Rogers.

Bradford is about 8 miles long and 3 wide, and contains about 10,000 acres, and 1650 inhabitants.

The soil is generally good and sufficiently various for

the cultivation of most productions common to this latitude. The town is bounded on one side its whole length by the Merrimack, a most beautiful river, whose waters afford considerable quantities of salmon, shad, bass, sturgeon, alewives and a variety of other fish. And in the spring there is a vast number of seines employed in taking these inhabitants of the flood. The salmon caught here are esteemed the best of any taken in the waters of the northern states, and often fetch from 75 to 100 cents a pound in the market at Boston. The quantity of fish is at present much less than formerly. To an admirer of the works and ways of God, hardly any thing can be more interesting than what is called the run of eels in this river. This generally takes place between the two run of shad. They go up the river the beginning of May, in a ribband or stream of about a foot wide upon the average, and three or four inches in depth, and every year in the same course. They are from two to six inches in length, move with considerable velocity, and continue to pass along without interruption for about four days ; almost an inconceivable number must pass during this time ; they are from the salt water, but how far they go up or what becomes of them I have not yet learned.

And now when upon the subject of the river, I think it proper to observe, that though in various ways this town in common with others upon its brinks, derive great advantages from this noble stream, it is obvious to any person who will take the trouble to reflect upon the subject, that these advantages are much less than they might, indeed ought to be. I will mention among other things, that while there is not probably a more convenient place in the county of Essex for the lumber trade, nor one where, from local circumstances enterprise and industry in that business, would with more certainty be crowned with success than is afforded upon its banks in this parish ; yet it is a fact, that for the want of such an establishment, the people, even in this town, to say nothing of Boxford,

Rowley, West Newbury, Andover, &c. are often put to inconvenience for articles of this description. And the same observation may be extended to the heavy articles of foreign merchandize, such as salt, molasses, sugar, iron, &c. It would be easy to refer to other particulars. But it is hoped this observation will draw the attention of some enterprising person of our town, or of some other place, to the subject.

The principal business done in this town, for many years after its settlement, was the cultivation of the land. And from the productive nature of the soil, the inhabitants had much encouragement to do this. Many of them set out large orchards, some of the trees in which grew to a great size. Several are spoken of and remembered, which in bearing years, yielded apples from which six and seven barrels of cider were made, and a few from eight to ten barrels. One of the largest of these was on land now owned by Mr. Jonathan Balch, a grandson of the first pastor of this church, by whom cider of a very superior quality was made, familiarly called *Arminian Cider*, and which for many years bore the highest price in market of any made in the state. Formerly there were considerable quantities of peaches and plumbs produced in this town, but for several years past, trees of this description have not flourished. There is however at present an apparent change for the better, and the present appearance is, that persons may now cultivate these trees with the hope of enjoying the fruit of them.

There was a time between the years 1700 and 1790, when less attention was paid to the cultivation of fruit, than the real interest of the town required, the stately trees which the fathers had planted, yield in great abundance, and the inhabitants seem hardly to have thought these could ever fail, and were therefore less careful to provide for those that should come after them, than their fathers had been before. At the present there is an increased attention to this subject, several very fine young orchards of engrafted fruit now ornament our town.

The winter pear, formerly called the Warden pear, was introduced into this town by Mr. ———— Wooster, brother to Francis Wooster, grandfather of Samuel Worcester, D. D. of Salem, a man who from his singular ingenuity, was familiarly called doctor. But whether he cultivated this pear from the Dummer trees in Byfield, or imported it, cannot be certainly ascertained, though the last is the most probable.

*Trade and Manufactories.* The first store of any considerable importance in this town was opened by Moses Parker, Esq. who for many years did business to a considerable extent, and whose store, it is said, was furnished with a very great variety of merchandize. There are now about seven or eight stores of greater or less extent in which may be had most of the articles required in common life, and upon as good terms as in any other place in this part of the county.

Ship building has been and would still be, were it not for the present depressed state of commerce, a very important branch of business here ; ships of rising four hundred tons may be safely launched. And with what is publicly known on the subject, it will not appear a matter of boasting, to say, our ship carpenters are well taught and skilful mechanics. The business was commenced by Mr. John Atwood, from Boston, in 1720.

The manufactory of leather is carried on to considerable extent, five tan yards are now in full operation. This business was first commenced by Shubel Walker, in the upper parish, in the early settlement of this town, but is now almost entirely confined to the east parish.

Large quantities of shoes are manufactured here, and sent to the southern and middle states, the West Indies, &c. About 150 men are constantly employed in this business, beside many who employ the winter in it, who it is supposed make 50,000 pairs of shoes and boots yearly. This business as a trade, furnishing shoes for market, was commenced by Daniel Hardy, now of Pelham, about sixty years since, who used to send his shoes to Portsmouth. He was followed by Thomas Savory, Esq. and Nathaniel Mitchell, who carried on the business extensively, sending their shoes to the southern states, and to the West Indies. About the time of the French revolution, Moses Savory and a Mr. Gage, went in the same business, from which time it has been one of the most important articles in the business of this town.

In 1798, William Tenny, Jr. commenced chaise making, since which time considerable has been done at that business, and is now doing, and perhaps never by more skilful and industrious mechanics than at present.

Thomas Carlton, about the year 1760, set up a fulling mill on Johnson's creek, above Aaron Parker's upper mill where he carried on the dressing of cloth. In this factory Mr. Benjamin Morse partly learned the trade, who in connection with his sons, has for many years, and to a considerable extent, carried on the business, and in a manner creditable to themselves and much to the public satisfaction.

A small quantity of chocolate, was about thirty years since, manufactured by Jesse Atwood.

Brass and pewter buckles and sleigh bells, were to a considerable amount made here by Stephen Foster, and others for some years before and after the revolution. Nothing however is done at this business now.

Coopering business has been carried on in this town at different times to a greater or less extent, very little however has been done at it for some years. This business is about to be revived by Jotham Hunt, who is making preparations for that purpose. During the revolutionary war, salt petre was made in this place by Deacon Samuel Tenny.

In 1800, was commenced the manufactory of Straw Bonnets, which is now carried on to a considerable extent in this town, and much to the advantage of those who are employed in it.

A considerable quantity of Tobacco is manufactured in this town. This business was commenced in 1770, by Moses Parker, Esq. a man excelled by few in real mechanical powers of mind. When he commenced this business, he was but about thirteen years of age, and never had enjoyed but one opportunity of seeing the machinery used in this work.

*Mines, &c.*—I have not learned that any other than iron mine has been known to exist in this place, of this there is apparently a large quantity in the east part of the town.

Clay of different qualities is found in many parts of the town, suitable for the common purposes for which it is used. There is one bed in the east part of the town, of a finer quality, which I have reason to believe might be worked to advantage in making the finer articles of the Potter.

There are two springs in the east parish, one on the land of Thomas Savory, Esq. the other on that of Isaiah Jewitt, the waters of which are empregnated with iron, and if properly improved and secured from other water, might no doubt be used to advantage by persons afflicted with disorders for which calybiate waters are prescribed.

It being the opinion of some who professed to have knowledge and experience on the subject, that there was mineral coal and lead in the hill between the east meeting house and the river, an attempt was made to ascertain the fact in 1808, and a considerable time and property expended, but without success. But I can hardly suppose any one acquainted with mining, would from looking at what was done, consider this failure as any very positive evidence that there is none there.

*Mills, &c.*—Johnson's creek affords the greatest and indeed the only considerable means for water works in this town, and it has been considerably improved for this purpose, for on it have stood, or are now standing, four saw mills, five grist mills, three fulling mills, two bark mills.

The first of these was a grist mill, standing below the road leading from Mr. Daniel Kimball's to deacon Thomas Morse's, and was set up by Edward Carlton, the first person born in Rowley, or his father, probably about the year 1670. This mill is not now standing, nor is the place where it stood occupied. In 1780, deacon Phineas Carlton, built a mill lower down the stream, just on the opposite side of the creek from that on which Mr. Aaron Parker's upper mill now stands, and had the sluice dug which is now in repair. This was done, by job for 70 dollars, by Cuff Dole, a person of color, of remarkable strength, steady habits, and who died in the comfortable hope of a blessed immortality.

In 1750, Joseph Kimball and Eliphalet Hardy, set up the lower mill so called, and as it was a work of considerable magnitude to build the damn, and the mill greatly needed, the inhabitants volunteered their services, some men only of common property, subscribing and afterwards performing from fifteen to twenty days labor.

In 1790, Retier Parker built a tanyard near the lower mill, and contrived to have the stone with which the bark is ground, moved by water instead of horses, as was the practice at that time, certainly a useful improvement.

All these, with the exception of a part of the lower mill, have become the property of Aaron Parker, Esq. a man of ingenuity and enterprise, who has improved them in a manner highly creditable to himself, and to the advantage and convenience of the public. He has also attached a rolling and fulling mill, to his upper grist mill, and has a bark mill running with such perfection, that it will grind as much bark in two hours, as could be ground in a whole day by the former mill, though as we observed, that was a great improvement upon the general practice of the day.

In 1684, this town received proposals from Richard Whomes, of Rowley, and John Perle, of Marblehead, to set up a corn mill upon this creek, a little above the mill built by the first Mr. Carlton, which proposals were well received by the town, and considerable subscriptions were made to forward the design, upon condition, that said Whomes and Perle would set up a good and sufficient mill, and that the people in this town should be served in their turn, in preference to those from out of town, and also that sufficient passage be left for fish, which conditions were agreed to, and the mill accordingly set up. This mill is not standing at present.

The first saw mill was owned by the Carlton family, but when built I have not learned. It must have been in the early settlement of the town. It stood across the road above the place of the first grist mill. And it is a fact worthy of notice, that the mud sills of the three first mills are still remaining, and can be seen, though it must be about 150 years, perhaps more, since they were put down.

In 1784, Mr. Francis Kimball built a saw mill, and Mr. Benjamin Morse a fulling mill near the mouth of the creek, the latter of which is now standing and in full operation.

Besides these, there have been five or six saw mills in different parts of the town, and one grist mill, upon temporary streams. One of the saw mills on the farm of David How, has recently been put in good repair.

I shall take this opportunity to observe, that though much use is made of the water of Johnson's creek, yet a much more considerable advantage might be derived from it. Several mills more might with perfect convenience stand upon it. The convenience of the public does certainly call for the erection of a carding mill. Another saw mill would find full employ, indeed it would be easy to show how enterprising individuals might get wealth, and the community be better served, by enlisting in their service, the force of this water which God in his goodness causes to flow down this stream for the use of men.

*Roads, &c.* The first committee upon record, for laying out highway in this town, were sergeant John Gage, Joseph Pike, John Griffin, who were appointed in the year 1668. How far these persons were concerned in laying out our roads, it is impossible for us now to say. It is certain, whoever were the agents in this business, they committed an error in making them so narrow; an inconvenience greatly felt, but which I am happy to observe, the town is taking measures, as far as may be, to remedy. Several have already been widened in part, and have been given orders for the widening others. Though this measure will be attended with considerable expense and labor, it will, beyond doubt, be ultimately found a measure of economy as well as beauty and convenience. Our roads, though narrow, are, in general, well made, and the bridges all in good repair. And I cannot but think that a stranger passing through this town, will from the state of the roads, the good order in our public houses, the appearance of our fields, and the beauty of the river, find as much to entertain the mind and please their fancy, as in most towns in this county.

It was the early policy of this town, and a good policy it is, to restrain cattle, &c. In order to carry this regulation into effect, as well as for other obvious purposes, they voted the 5th of January, 1685, to build a pound, with gate, lock and key, to be set up the next spring, on such part of the meeting-house land, as the selectmen should judge most convenient, which order was carried into effect. The present pound occupies a different place, and was built after the west parish built their present meeting.house, who seem, for some reason unknown to me, to have had the expense of this to defray.

At the same meeting in which the vote passed to call this town Bradford, instructions were given to the selectmen, to provide a burying-ground, who, it seems, were furnished with the land now improved for that purpose, in the west parish, by the liberality of John Haseltine, Jr. of Haverhill, upon condition the town would keep it fenced, which condition was however, the same year given up by his son Samuel, of Bradford; so the town now holds it without condition.

The burying ground in this part of the town, is a present to the parish, from Mr. Samuel Jewitt, and the first person buried there was Mrs. Martha Hale, in 1723. As we learn from the inscription on the stone at the foot,

> If you will look, it may appear
> She was the first that was buried here.

*Schools, &c.*—There is much reason to suppose, this town was furnished with schools in part, at the public expense, and that the provision for these, was among the "prudentials" intrusted to the selectmen, from the earliest date. There is however, no vote of the town recorded on this subject, till the year 1701, when it was voted, the selectmen should provide a school, according to their discretion, and that they should assess the town for the expense of the same. The next year it was voted that those who sent to school, should pay two pence a week for those that learned to read, and four pence for those that learned to write, the additional expense to be paid by the town. The person's name who kept, was Ichabods, the next whose name is mentioned, was Master White, who commenced in 1723, and received 24*l*. 10*s*. a year. His successor was Hobey, who was followed by a Mr. Merrel. All these persons kept through the year, and most of them for several years each, and as far as we can judge, were well qualified for the business.

The first school-house was built on the meeting-house land, 22 feet long, 18 feet wide and 7 feet posts, and cost 25*l*. The building committee, were Jonathan Woodman, sergeant Robert Haseltine and Nathaniel Walker.

There are at present seven school-houses in six districts, in which are kept twenty four months of man's school annually, and in summer there is good provision made for the instruction of small children.

In June 7, 1805, the town accepted a report made by their committee appointed for that purpose, consisting of Moses Parker, Daniel Stickney, Bradstreet Parker, Thomas Savory, Esq. and Samuel Tenny, for the better management of the town school. The regulations recommended in this report, have, by experiment, been found good and useful; and under the advantages now afforded the children and youth, for the acquisition of knowledge, competent to the common concerns of life, they are certainly making very encouraging progress. And I do not think I am influenced by prejudice, or judge without some knowledge on the subject when I say that I have never known children in common life, so forward in learning, as those in the districts which come under my immediate inspection. And as the regulations through town, are the same, it is presumed the same observation may be extended to all.

It would be an additional improvement, both in regard to economy and the advancement of our children, were the committee empowered to prescribe in all cases, the books which should be used. And there can be but little doubt, but the same observation would hold true in regard to the towns furnishing the necessary stationary to be used in schools.

The greatest inconvenience, we experience, is the unequal division of the school districts, an evil which I do not know can well be remedied; but being an evil which all now feel, will I hope, teach all that in the course of years, individuals can be benefitted in no surer way, than by consulting the general good.

Beside these public schools, there is an academy in the west parish, founded in 1803, and chiefly supported by inhabitants living in that part of the town. This institution has, for several years past, enjoyed a large share of public patronage, the best evidence we can have of its being esteemed, by those who have no motives for partiality, a good institution. God has also sent his blessings upon it. Several considerable revivals of religion have taken place there among the students, and many, who came in pursuit of human science, have there learned that fear of the Lord, which is the beginning of wisdom, and acquired that good understanding, which all have who keep his commandments. Near 2500 youth have received instruction within its walls; numbers of whom have performed or are now performing parts in the theatre of life, honorable to themselves, and useful to the world. Among whom, you will not expect, I should fail to name, Mrs. Harriet Newell, who in life, took a part in carrying the gospel to a land shadowing in darkness, and whose writings, published since her death, have been the happy instrument of exciting the attention of many, to the obligations they owe to the heathen world.

This academy is under the direction of eleven trustees, viz:—Rev. Jonathan Allen, A. M. Pres. Rev. Isaac Braman, Col. James Kimball, Mr. Edward Kimball, Joseph Chadwick, Esq. Rev. Joshua Dodge, Dea. John Hasseltine, Mr. Moses Kimball, Hon. John Varnum, Rev. Gardner B. Perry, Mr. William Tenny, and has funds to the amount of about two thousand dollars.

Since its foundation, the following persons have held the place of principal instructors in the two apartments. Rev. Samuel Walker, Rev. Samuel Guile, Rev. Abraham Burnham, Samuel Morrell, Samuel Peabody, Daniel Hardy, Luther Baily, Hon. Samuel Adams, Richard Kimball, Rev. Ebenezer P. Sperry, Nathaniel Dike, Joseph Noyes, and Benjamin Greenleaf the present preceptor.

In the female apartment, Miss Hannah Swan, Mary Boardman, Harriet Webster, Betsey Allen, Charlotte

Gage, Abigail C. Hasseltine, the present preceptress.*

There are two libraries in this town, in which there is a respectable number of well chosen books, besides several little collections owned by small associations.

The Washington Benevolent Society, is an institution now exclusively devoted to literary improvement, and the business is conducted, as I have much reason to suppose, in a manner highly useful to the members. And I must say with its present cast, it is highly desirable, that the young men should more generally become members of it. It is by no means designed, and it is far from being desirable, that it should be confined to one part of the town, though hitherto most of its members have been of this parish. And I cannot but think, that the young men, who do not avail themselves of the advantages of this or some similar institution, will, in the course of a few years, find themselves considerably behind those in real information, who every month assemble for improvement in useful knowledge.

The following persons have received a public education—

| Years. | Names. | Colleges. | Residence. |
| --- | --- | --- | --- |
| 1698 | Rev. Thomas Symmns, **A. M.** | *Harvard*, | Bradford, *dec.* |
| 1736. | Rev. Samuel Webster, S. T. D. | *Harvard*, | Salisbury, Ms. *dec.* |
| 1774. | Rev. Benj. Thurston, A. M. | *Harvard*, | Exeter, N. H. *dec.* |
| 1782. | Benj. Parker, **A** M. M.D, M.M.S.Soc. | *Harvard*, | Bradford, |
| 1789. | Daniel Hardy, Jr. A. M. | *Dartmouth*, | Pelham. N. H. |
| 1790 | Samuel Walker, Esq. | *Harvard*, | Rutland, Vt. |
| 1794. | Aaron Hardy, A. M. | *Dartmouth*, | Boston, *dec.* |
| 1800 | John Dutch, | *Dartmouth*, | Bradford, |
| 1800. | Rev. Daniel Kimball, A. M. | *Harvard*, | Hingham, Ms. |
| 1803 | Rev. David T. Kimball, A. M. | *Harvard*, | Ipswich, Ms. |
| 1804. | Leonard Kimball, A. M. | *Harvard*, | Baltimore, |
| 1808 | Nathaniel K Hardy, | *Dartmouth*, | Pembroke, *dec.* |
| 1808. | Frederic Muzzy, Esq. | *Columbia*, | N. York City, *dec.* |
| 1810. | Richard Kimball, A. M. | *Dartmouth*, | Ipswich, Ms. |
| 1812. | George Parker, A M. | *Harvard*, | Southward, |
| 1815. | Rev. Alonzo Phillips, A. M. | *Middlebury*, | Princeton, Ms. |
| 1815 | Rev. David Tenny, A. M. | *Harvard*, | Missionary, *dec.* |
| 1820 | James Kimball, Jr. | *Middlebury*, | Andover, |
| 1821. | Stephen Morse, | *Dartmouth*, | Bradford. |

* It may not be improper to notice, that since this discourse was written, a building has been erected in the east parish, designed among other useful purposes, for an academy, in which it is hoped to afford youth, who may resort here, the common advantages of such institutions.

*Title to the Soil, &c.*—So far as the government of the colony was concerned, we have already seen, that our ancestors became in rightful possession of the land, in virtue of the patent granted to Mr. Rogers. And the settlement was made according to the acknowledgement of his descendants, with the full " knowledge, license and liking " of *Maschonomontic, alias Maschonnomit, the chief Sagamore and native proprietor of all the land between the Merrimack and Naumkeag or Bass rivers. But there was no actual purchase of the land from him. In consequence of this, his descendants and heirs, Samuel English and Joseph English, grand-children, and John Umpee, his nephew, set up a claim to the soil in 1700, which claim was allowed by the town, and a committee consisting of John Tenny, Joseph, Bailey, Richard Kimball, Sen. Phillip Atwood and John Boynton, was chosen the 23d of November that year, to treat with these persons, and purchase the land at the town's expense. This they did for the sum of 6*l.* 10 shillings, and took a deed for the land, signed by these three persons, dated 13th January 1701. Samuel English putting down for his mark, the sign of a serpent, Joseph English, that of a bow and arrow, and John Umpee, that of a new moon.

Those therefore, who now possess landed property here, may comfort themselves with the reflection, that so far as the original possessors are concerned, they have a just title to it, a reflection which must yield no small satisfaction to those who wish to do justly by all. In consequence as it is presumed, of the wise and equitable dealings of the first settlers, and their immediate descendants, with the aboriginal inhabitants, next to the restraining influence of God's spirit, the people in this town were never much molested by them. I have found

* Maschonnomit, or as it is spelt in some other records, Maschanomet, was one of the five Sagamores, who in 1643, signed an instrument by which they put themselves and people under the government of the Massachusetts Colony.

but one record of any violence experienced from them. This is contained in a note attached to one of the town books, by Shubel Walker, who was then town clerk, a man admirably fitted for that office, being a very fine writer, and very accurate in the duties of his office; he served the town several years. He observes in this note, that Thomas Kimball, was shot by an Indian, the 3d of May, 1676, and his wife and five children, Joannah, Thomas, Joseph, Prescilla and John, were carried captive. These however, he observes in another note, returned home again the 13th of June the same year. Mr. Kimball's house stood on the road leading to Boxford, between Mr. Nathaniel Woodman's and Mr. Peabody's, about twenty rods towards Boxford, where the well and cellar still remain. It is traditionally reported, that the Indians, who committed this violence, set out from their homes, near Dracutt, with the intention of killing some one in Rowley, who they supposed had injured them, but finding the night too far spent, they did not dare to proceed further, and so avenged themselves on Mr. Kimball, for an injury another man had done them. There was also a Mr. Nehemiah Carlton, shot from across the river, at the time of the attack upon Haverhill. And it is said farther, that one of the workmen employed in felling timber on the Haverhill side of the river, for building the house now owned by Reuben Carlton, was also shot. Beside these I have heard of no particular injury received from them. There must have been a considerable settlement of Indians in this town, as is evident from the number of bones found in and about the hill near Paul Parker's. The last of these who resided here, was Papahana, who lived to a great age, in a hut near the mouth of Johnson's creek; the people of the last generation, knew him well. The name of the tribe to which this settlement belonged, is not certainly known, but is supposed to be the Pawtucet.

There were three garrison houses built at an early period in this town, one of brick at the west end of the town, near the place where Mr. John Day's house now stands. One where the parsonage was afterwards built, opposite the burying-ground, in the west parish. The third where widow Rebecca Foster's house is; this was palisaded. The inhabitants of the town, often passed the night in these houses, when from any circumstance they apprehended danger from the savages. There was also a block house on the neck so called, near the falls, in which, during times of danger, the inhabitants watched by turns.

*Town Officers.*—One thing which contributes greatly to the respectability, the moral habits, and indeed to the prosperity of a town, is the appointment of suitable men to transact its public concerns. And I am happy to observe, that the records of this town, carry with them strong internal evidence, that such has been the character of a very great proportion of the men, who have, at different periods, had the conducting of its affairs. In the early settlement of the town, the selectmen appeared to have been considered the fathers of the town; and accordingly were from year to year, for a great period, empowered by the town, to manage all its "prudential affairs according to the best of their discretion." And if any opinion can be gathered from the town records, they merited the confidence placed in them. I do not find an instance, in which there is the least evidence of any dissatisfaction on the part of the town, for what they did, unless the raising a school committee in the year     to manage the concerns of the schools, which had, before this, been left with the selectmen, was such. The first who served in this office, were sergeant John Gage, Robert Hasseltine, Joseph Pike, John Griffin, John Tenny. Agreeable to the discretionary power entrusted to the selectmen, we find them giving directions concerning the height of fences, &c., things now regulated by law.

And as I perhaps shall not find a more convenient place, I will observe here, that Thomas Kimball was at the first meeting in this town, chosen constable, Samuel Wooster, Benjamin Gage, Benjamin Kimball, David Hasseltine, overseers, Joseph Pike, clerk. And at the same meeting, it was voted, that the houses of Benjamin Gage and Thomas Kimball, " should be legal places for posting up any order or other business of public concernment to the whole town." And this remained the order of the town, for any thing that appears, with the exception of one year, when the meeting-house was made the place for such notifications, till the division of the town into parishes. I mention this because it makes known the parts of the town, which were then the places of most resort and most business. And also as an evidence that the people of those days, thought the setting up such notifications on meeting-houses to be read sabbath days, was bringing religious and secular things too much together.

In 1707, the town voted there should be two constables instead of one, as before, chosen from the two parts of the town, and that the twenty-five shillings that had been given yearly for this service, should be divided between them. This is the first act of the town, which looks like any acknowledgement of a claim to public notice, from local circumstances, and was the commencement of a practice, in regard to town offices, which has prevailed to the present time, and by which the two parts of the town have acted together with a great degree of harmony and good feeling, and which I earnestly hope they will ever continue to do. And it was this measure which led the way in the division of the town into parishes, which took place about twenty years after.

*Public Order.*—There are few circumstances in the lives of men, better calculated to give a correct view of their character, than their regard to public order. And

I am happy to find, that a commendable regard to this, is evident in all the doings of this town. At the first. meeting, it was voted "that whoever did not appear at town meeting, at the time set for such meeting, should pay six pence for every hour he was "defective," and if any one in meeting should speak without leave obtained from the moderator, he should pay the same sum for every "offence." On the 11th of January, 1668, "it was further voted, that when the town are assembled in town meeting, that no one should leave the house without liberty obtained, under the penalty of twelve pence per hour, and that no act passed by the town after sunset shall be of value."

In March 1699, a vote was passed to preserve order in the meeting-house, and for this purpose it was ordered, that seats should be assessed to individuals, and that if any should refuse to take the seat assigned him, after proper notice, he should be fined five shillings for every day of public assembly, from which vote there were but two dissenting voices, viz: Joseph and Jacob Hardy. In 1708, when the new meeting-house was to be seated, the town instructed the committee appointed for that purpose, to place the men above 60, according to their age, and all others according to their rates, having no respect to the rates of sons and servants.

In 1818, a vote was passed unanimously in this parish, recommending to all, to go into the meeting-house during the tolling of the bell on days of public worship, and also to make as little noise as practicable in moving the falling seats. I refer to this as an evidence, that the people retain the same good ideas of public order, which so highly recommends the first settlers in this town, and to remind those who may have forgotten this resolve, that it stands yet, as the expression of the sense of the parish, concerning what is decent to be done in and about the house of God. And it is pleasing to observe, that there appears to be an increasing attention to the recommendation contained in this vote.

*Health.*—Bradford has been as much favoured in this respect, as towns in general. So far as is known, there never has been a specifick local disorder here; as far back as we have records, about one in ten of the deaths has been of persons rising eighty years; for the few years past the proportion has been rather greater. In this parish since my settlement, full one, out of eight of the deaths, has been of those, who, by reason of strength, had lived to four score years; and I am happy to say, that in most of these, old age was honourable, because found in the ways of righteousness.

In 1736, this town, in common with several other parts of New England, was visited with the throat distemper, which in one year, carried off in this parish, forty-seven children, and nine grown persons. And it is said that only two families entirely escaped the disorder, one of which was that of their Rev. Pastor. And I apprehend it is from this circumstance, connected with the French war, so called, which made another draft upon persons of the same generation, that there are fewer persons of from 86 and upwards living now, than there was in the former generation, and less than there is a prospect of being in the generation now following them, in this county, and perhaps in other parts of New-England. This appears to me, at least, a much more probable reason for the present diminution among aged people, than the one generally given, that people do not now live as long, as in the early settlement of the country.

In 1762, the throat distemper returned again, when about twenty-three were taken away by it, in a short time. And in 1794, fifteen more died of the same disorder. May God, in his great mercy, forbid that this judgment should return any more to this place. May the rising generation be *saved from the pestilence which*

*walketh in darkness, and from the distruction which wasteth
at noon-day.*

In May 1777, the small-pox made its appearance in
this place. The first person that died with it, was Jeremiah Hardy. The town built a pest house on the road
passing by Mr. Benjamin Jaquis's, south of his house,
and removed those to it, who had taken the disorder.
Fourteen had the disorder and ten died. Just about the
time those, who recovered, were permitted to return to
their homes, the pest house was consumed by fire ; but
the town, though it instituted an enquiry, was not able
to ascertain by what means the fire was communicated
to it.

What is called the revolution in this country, and by
which we became a free and independent people, is a
subject of so much general interest, the young will be
glad to be informed, and the old to be reminded, what
part this town took, in that glorious and ever memo-
rable affair. The first public measure upon record, is
the choice of captain Daniel Thurston, in 1774, to set
in the provincial congress, which was to meet at Con-
cord the 11th of October, that year. And at a subse-
quent meeting of the freeholders and other inhabitants
of the town of Bradford, duly warned and legally assembled, it was voted to give to captain Daniel Thurston, the representative of the town of Bradford, in general assembly, the following instructions. " Sir, we, his
majesty's most dutiful and loyal subjects, freeholders and
other inhabitants of the town of Bradford, in town meeting legally assembled, this 7th of January 1775, take
this opportunity to express our very great uneasiness,
at the infringements of our natural and constitutional
rights, by many of the late measures of the British administration ; particularly those of the taxation of the
colonies, and the granting of salaries to the judges of
the Superior Court, measures adapted as we apprehend,
to lay a foundation in time, to render property preca-

rious and to introduce a system of despotism, which we cannot view, but with the utmost aversion, and to which we cannot submit, while possible to be avoided. We recommend it to you as our representative in general assembly, to use your influence to obtain redress of all our injuries ; and in particular to enquire whether the support of the judges of the Superior Court, has been adequate to their services, office and station ; and if not, to use your influence in obtaining suitable grants and establishments, as may be thought sufficient to remove all pretence, that government is not sufficiently supported among ourselves, which was voted unanimously. We also vote the thanks of this town, to the town of Boston, for the care and vigilance they have discovered for the rights and privileges of this province, as men, as christians, and as subjects. Voted, that the town clerk, be directed to transmit a copy of these instructions, &c. to the committee of correspondence in Boston."

<table>
<tr><td>Dudley Carlton,<br>William Greenough,<br>Benjamin Gage, Jr.<br>Thomas Webster,<br>Amos Mulliken.</td><td>} Committee to make report.</td></tr>
</table>

As the difficulties between this and the mother country increased, and it had become a serious question, whether the united colonies should declare themselves independent, a meeting of the town was called "to see whether the town would advise or give Dudley Carlton, their representative, any instructions relative to the honourable congress declaring the United Colonies independent states." And the town met accordingly on the 20th of June 1776, when they appointed Thomas Webster, John Burbank, capt. Nathaniel Gage, Benjamin Muzzy, John Savory, to consult and report to the meeting, what ought to be done ; which committee reported, that they should send to their representative the following instructions, viz:

To Dudley Carlton, Esq. representative from the town of Bradford, in general assembly,

"Sir—When we consider the despotick plan of government, adopted by the king, ministry and parliament of Great Britain, to enslave these American colonies. When we consider, instead of redressing our grievances, they have turned a deaf ear to the repeated petitions and remonstrances of all the United Colonies, and have also been and are still endeavoring to enforce their arbitrary plan upon us, by spilling our blood, by burning our towns, by seizing our property and by instigating the savages of the wilderness, and the negroes to take up the cause against us. When we consider these things, it raises our indignation, that we who have always been loyal subjects to the king of Great Britain, should be so unconstitutionally and inhumanly treated; such tyranical impositions and abuses of power, we cannot as men submit to. Therefore utterly despairing of a happy reconciliation ever taking place between Great Britian and these colonies, you are hereby desired, as our representative, to use your utmost endeavour, that our delegates in general congress be instructed to shake off the tyrannical yoke of Great Britain, and declare these United Colonies independent of that venal, corrupt and avaricious court forever, provided no proposals for a happy reconciliation be offered, which the honorable congress think proper to accept, and we hereby engage that we will, at the risk of our lives and fortunes, endeavour to defend them therein."

Which report was accepted so far as it appears unanimously, and accordingly sent.

This town united also by unanimous vote, in the exertions which were made through this state, to procure an universal observance of an act of the state, to prevent monopoly: And at the same meeting, gave the selectmen discretionary power to purchase guns and powder. In the same year they met to choose some one firmly attached to the American cause, to secure this and the other United States, against the danger to which they were exposed by internal enemies, and Abraham Day, Jr. was made choice of for this purpose. As it would not be possible to go through all the measures the town took in this work, I will remark that during the continuance of the war, the people of the town appear to have been ready and willing to do their part in the toil, and bear their part of the expenses of that war; which remark is abundantly supported by their numerous votes to raise money, provision and men, whenever called upon by the proper authorities, and from their prompt assistance, without any call, when the exigencies of the country seemed to require.

After the cessation of hostilities, when this country had virtually obtained the object contended for, it became a question, what course should be taken in regard to those who had left the country during the war. The sentiment of this town on the subject, may be learned from the following resolution, passed May 17th, 1783, viz: " That the representative from this town the ensuing year, be instructed to use his utmost endeavour, to prevent any person or persons returning to live in this commonwealth, who have conspired against or absented themselves from the United States, during the continuance of the war with Great Britain." The sentiment expressed in this vote, prevailed generally at that time, but has not borne the test of more cool deliberation.

After the declaration of independence, it became a subject of great concern, to define the principles and fix upon the form of government in this commonwealth. And there were measures taken to get the minds of the people, on the subject of a new constitution, and of the manner it should be formed. The result this town

came to, is expressed in the following resolution, " that
we are not willing, nor do we consent, that the house
of representatives and council acting in one body, as
proposed in a resolve of the house, passed September
17, 1776, should agree on, and enact a constitution, and
form of government for this state, but we are willing
and do desire that the honourable council, and the honourable house of representatives, each acting in their
respective capacities proceed to form a plan of government for this state, and exhibit attested copies of the
same, to the several towns, for their inspection and ap-
probation, before it be ratified and confirmed."

In 1779, when delegates were to be chosen for the
formation of a constitution, this town made choice of
Peter Russel, Esq. to meet with the convention, to be
assembled for that purpose on the 1st of September,
and instructed him, when the constitution was formed,
to deliver a copy of it to the selectmen, in order to have
it laid before the town for their inspection. The constitution being formed and sent to the people in 1780,
the people voted to accept it, requiring however, that
the word *protestant* should be inserted after the word
christian in the qualification for governor. There were
eleven votes against the third article, the rest appears to
have been adopted without dissent.

In 1795, when the time had arrived for the revision of
the constitution, according to a provision made in it, if
the people desired it, there was but one vote in favour
of a revision.

This year, as you know, there has been a new pro-
posal for alteration, arising professedly from this circumstance, that one large portion of this state has been separated from it. A majority of votes was given in favor
of revision. And there being found to be a majority in
the state, this town voted to send to the Convention, and
for this purpose, made choice of Daniel Stickney, and
Jesse Kimball, Esquires. The Convention is now in

session, and the revision going on perhaps not with all the speed the public expected, but with a spirit and talent which promises a happy issue.

*Religion.*—At what time the people upon this river, began first to enjoy the worship of God by themselves, does not appear from any record that I have found. Rev. Mr. Zechariah Symmes, must have resided in this town in capacity of a religious teacher, at least about fourteen years before his ordination. For in the first legal town meeting of which we have a record, held in 1668, it was voted, that the selectmen chosen that year, should have power to carry on and finish the minister's house according to Mr. Symmes' direction, though he was not ordained till 1682. And for his support, the first year, he received forty pounds, the next year fifty, which appears to have been his yearly salary, till the time of his ordination. The one half of this was to be paid in wheat, pork, butter and cheese, the other half in malt, indian corn or rye. And the town appear to have been desirous to make his circumstances altogether comfortable, for in 1669, they voted to defray the expense of bringing his goods to town, gave him forty acres of land near Indian hill, and appointed sergeant Gage, John Simmons and David Haseltine, to lay it out. And further appointed Robert Haseltine and Samuel Wooster, to gather the tax, and take care to have Mr. Symmes' work done, and to attend to such other things as he should stand in need of during the year. And a committee was appointed for the same purpose from year to year, during his and the greater part of his successor's ministry in this place. Indeed provision for the full and respectable enjoyment of religion, and for the comfort of those who ministered to them in holy things, formed a very prominent trait in the character of the first settlers in this town. Hardly a meeting of the town passed without doing something on this subject, and all manifesting a liberality which does them honor. In accordance with what was a princi-

pal object with them, they appointed in 1677, Samuel
Wooster, John Tenny, John Simmons and Richard Hall,
to join with Mr. Symmes "to advise to what might be
thought best for the further carrying on the affairs of religion, and to prepare for the settlement of the ordinances
of God, in this place." And in 1681, it was voted and
consented to, "that the Rev. Mr. Symmes have liberty at
his discretion, to call out any two men of the inhabitants
of the town, to assist him in catechising the youth, and
also to go with him to see who of the heads of the families or others, would join the church." That the last part
of this resolve may be understood, it may be necessary
to observe, that it was now in contemplation to form a
church in this town, for though the inhabitants of this
town had enjoyed, as we have noticed, the ministry of
the word, they had not the holy sacrament, for their religious teacher, Mr. Symmes, had not yet been ordained ;
the pious were united with the church at Rowley, Haverhill, and perhaps with other neighboring societies,
the object therefore of this resolution was to see who
would take up their connections with other churches, and
unite in forming one in this place, and further to ascertain
whether there were not other serious persons disposed
to unite with them. Having ascertained each other's
feelings on this subject, and found, as their consequent
doings prove, the minds of professors favourable to such
a plan, they called in the pastors of several churches
to advise with them about the propriety of the measure
they had in contemplation. The result of their deliber-
ations we have in the following instrument.

"The question being proposed to us whose names are
under-written, whether the minister and people at Bradford, should promote without delay a coalition of themselves into a church and society, we answer in the affirmative, provided that the people do their utmost in taking effectual care, that he that preaches the gospel among
them, live on the gospel according to 1 Cor. ix, 14, that

so he may provide for his own household, as 1 Tim., v, 2, provided also, that their present teacher accept of office work among them so long as he finds he can comfortably discharge his duty, in all the relations he stands to God, his people and in his family, and that when he finds he cannot discharge his said duties respectively, the people shall freely release him of his engagement to them, after leave of council taken in the case: for hereby is a door opened for the worker to work the whole work of God, as an officer of Christ in that place, as others in office do in their places according to the 1 Cor. xvi. 10, *for he worketh the work of God as I also do;* hereby also is a better opportunity both for the worker and those that are taught to walk in all the commandments and ordinances of God blameless: Luke i, 6. That they may be found walking in the truth as we have received commandment from the father, 2 John 4. Dated 31st Oct. 1682.

This was subscribed by the Rev. Elder John Higginson, William Hubbard, John Brak, Samuel Phillips, John Richerson, John Hale, Edward Payson. And at a legal town meeting, November 28, 1682, it was voted and granted, that this resolve of the Rev. Elders, be entered in the town book as what was ascented to by all the inhabitants in the town.

To the conditions proposed by these reverend Elders, the town made the reply contained in the following instrument, which also contains the call they made to Mr. Symmes, to settle with them.

" We, the inhabitants of Bradford, met together at a legal town meeting, 13th March, 1682, in thankfulness to God for his great mercy in setting up his sanctuary among us, do hereby engage ourselves, jointly and singly, and do engage our children after us, as far as we may, by our parental authority, to endeavor by our and their utmost power, to uphold the faithful ministry of the gospel of Jesus Christ, in this town of Bradford, so long as we and they shall live; and for the encouragement of the same, to contribute a liberal and honorable maintenance towards it, as the rule of the gospel doth require, to the utmost of our and their ability, which God shall be pleased to bless us and them with from time to time. And for the encouragement of our present minister, we do covenant and promise to give and allow to him, so long as he shall continue with us as our minister, the full sum of sixty pounds per annum, if God be pleased to preserve us in our present capacity, and for to be paid in our present state annually, as follows: the first half in wheat and pork, butter and cheese, allowing at least to this half, one pound of butter for every milch cow and one cheese for a family; the other half to be in malt, indian or rye, except what he willingly excepts in other pay; the first payment to be made the second Thursday in October, the other payment to be made the third Thursday in March; and if any unforeseen providence shall hinder, then to take the next convenient day the week following.

We further grant liberty to him, to improve for his best advantage, what land we shall accomplish or obtain for our ministry. We grant him also liberty to feed his herd of cattle on our lands during his abode with us, which shall have the same liberty as our own cattle have. We engage to procure for him, at our own charge besides the annual stipend, sufficient firewood every year in good cord wood, he allowing six pence per cord, to bring it seasonably and cord it up in his yard. We engage also to furnish him yearly with ten sufficient loads of good hay if he need them at price current among us, and to bring it in the summer time and also to supply him with sufficient fencing and good stuff which he may hereafter need, at a reasonable lay. We engage that there be convenient highways provided and legally stated, to the several parcels of land, which we have given him; as to the five acres of meadow and the forty acres of upland, we bought of Benjamin Kimball. We do also engage that two men shall be chosen from year to year for the comfortable carrying on of his affairs, and that these two men shall have power to require any man at two days warning, according to his proportion, to help carry on his necessary husbandry work. We also engage that these agreements, together with any legal town acts, confirming the annual stipend and other concerns of our present minister, be duly and truely, in manner and kind as above specified without trouble to himself.

This was voted and granted to be entered in the town's book, at a legal town meeting the 13th January, 1682, as attests, SHUBAL WALKER, *Recorder*."

During the time these things were doing by the town, those who intended to unite in church relation, were preparing themselves for this solemnity, as we learn from the following instrument, which they called an act of Pacification, viz:—

"We, whose names are subscribed, being awfully sensible that we live in an age, wherein, God hath in part, executed the dreadful threatenings to take place in the earth, and wherein satan the great makebate and author of contentions, doth by God's holy permission exceedingly rage even in the visible church of God, and wherein the wicked one is sowing the tares of discord almost in every christian society, (the sad effects of which, we who are the inhabitants of Bradford, have for some years past experimentally felt, and have yet the bitter remembrance thereof,) we being now (through the rich and undeserved mercy of God in Christ Jesus) under hopeful probability of setting up a church of Christ Jesus in Bradford, do take this occasion, as to express our hearty and unfeigned sorrow and humiliation for what unchristian differences have broken forth among us, to the dishonor of God's name, the grief of his Spirit and to the obstructing of the word and kingdom of

Jesus Christ among us, and to the hindering of our own peace and edification; so also in the name of God and by his gracious help, seriously and solemnly do engage and promise for the future to forgive and forget, to the utmost of our endeavors, all former unchristian animosities, distances, alienations, differences and contests, private or more public, personal or social that have risen among us, or between us and other people, to pass a general act of amnesty and oblivion upon them all, and not to speak of them to the defamation of each other at home in Bradford town, much less abroad in any other place, nor to repeat or revive them, unless called by scripture rule or lawful authority to mention them for the conviction or spiritual advantage of each other. Besides, we promise, through the grace of God, that in case God in his most wise and holy providence, should permit any offences for the future to break forth among us, (which we desire God, in his infinite mercy would prevent, as far as may be for his glory and our own good,) that we will then conscientiously endeavour to attend scripture rules for the healing and removing them, and those holy rules in particular Levit. xix, 17, 18, Math. xviii, 15, &c. and so bring no matter of grievance against each other, to our minister and to our church, but in a scriptural and orderly way and manner. That we may be helped inviolably to observe this our agreement, we desire the assistance of each other's mutual, both christian and church watch, that we may be monitors or as it were remembrancers to each other of this branch of our covenant; as also through instant and constant prayers of each other, that God would enable us carefully to observe this instrument of our pacification and our conditional obligation to church and order, that God's name may be honored by us, and we may experience God's commanding his blessing upon us, even life forevermore.—Private fast, April 20, 1682, then was this vote passed.''

Having thus as they hoped sanctified themselves, and all things being ready, they united together in fellowship the 27th of December 1682, the day Mr. Symmes was ordained. It is much to be regretted, that part of the covenant they took is missing. What remains I will present to you.

**By the power of his Holy Spirit, in the ministry of his word, whereby we have been brought to see our misery by nature, our inability to help ourselves, and our need of a Saviour the Lord Jesus Christ, to whom we desire now solemnly to give up ourselves, as to our only Redeemer, to keep us by his power unto salvation. And for the furtherance of the blessed work, we are now ready to enter into a solemn covenant with God and with one another, that is to say, we do give up ourselves unto God whose name alone is Jehovah, as the only true and living God, and unto the Lord Jesus Christ, his only son, who is the Saviour, Prophet, Priest and King of his church and Mediator of the covenant of grace and to his Holy Spirit to lead us into all truth and to bring us unto salvation at the last. We do also give up our offsprings unto God in Christ Jesus, avouching him to be our God and the God of our children, humbly desiring him to bestow upon us that grace, whereby both we and they may walk before him as becomes his covenant people forever. We do also give up ourselves one unto another in the Lord, according to the will of God, engaging ourselves to walk together as a right ordered church of Christ, in all the ways of his worship, according to the rules of his most holy word, promising in brotherly labor, faithfully to watch over one another's souls and to submit ourselves to the government of Christ in his church, attending upon all his holy administrations according to the order of the gospel, so far as God hath or may reveal it to us by his word and Spirit.

| | |
|---|---|
| Zacheriah Symmes, | Samuel Haseltine, |
| ⋈ Samuel Stickney, | John Hardy, |
| John Tenny, | Joseph Bailey, |
| John Simmonds, | Abraham Haseltine, |
| William Huchence, | ⋈ John Boynton, |
| Joseph Palmer, | John Walson, |
| David Haseltine, | Robert Haseltine, |
| Richard Hall, | ⋈ B. Kimball, |
| ⋈ Thomas West, | ⋈ Robert Savory. |

Mr. Symmes was the son of Zacheriah Symmes minister of Charlestown, who came from England. Of his mother, Mr. Johnson, whose name we have had occasion to mention, observes, "that she was a godly woman. Her courage exceeded her stature, she bore every difficulty with cheerfulness, and raised up her ten children to people the American wilderness." It seems that after this, she must have had three more, for Mr. Symmes' Epitaph gives him five sons and eight daughters.

Our Mr. Symmes was educated at Cambridge, and graduated in 1657. He must have been a man of considerable note as well as learning, for he was one of the fellows of Harvard College, and I believe preached an Election Sermon. Judging from the church records, we have much reason to suppose, that *he took heed to the ministry which he received of the Lord to fulfil it.* And the work of grace was carried on through his instrumentality; 126 were added to the church, and 238 were baptized during his ministry, which, considering the then population of the town, must be considered a goodly number. In 1705, as Mr. Symmes grew old and feeble, the town voted "to employ some one to help their beloved Pastor in the work of the ministry," and appointed Capt. David Haseltine and Ensign John Tenny, to go abroad and upon good information, invite some one to come and labor among them. This committee employed a Mr. Hale, who

⋈ The persons whose names have this mark prefixed to them, signed this covenant by putting their mark to it.

after a trial of a few Sabbaths, the town liked so well, they voted to employ him for a year, and to give him thirty pounds, his own board and horse keeping. The next year they voted to give him the same sum, and 50 shillings more instead of keeping his horse, and during the year made his support in all, equal to 46 pounds; and it seems upon the whole, they intended to have settled him, for something like an expression of this passed in town meeting, but why it was never accomplished is not known. In the year 1706, a difficulty arising between Mr. Symmes and the town, relative to some items in his salary, it was mutually agreed it should be left to council; and Dea. Tenny, Dea. Bailey and Phillip Atwood were appointed to manage the business before the council, and afterwards Capt. David Haseltine and Lieut. Richard Kimball were added to the committee, and for ought appears, the affair was amicably adjusted. Mr. Symmes was evidently greatly respected by the town, and his judgment much confided in. And it is nothing more than an act of justice to say, the town appear to have acted generously in the provision they made for his temporal comfort, and to have united readily with him in all his exertions to do good.

*Upon his tomb stone is the following Inscription.*

Conditum Hie Corpus Viri Veri Reverendi Zachaii Symmes College Harvardini Quondam Socii Evangelii Ministri Nati Omnigena Eruditione Ornati Pietate Vitaeque Sanctitate Maxime Conspicui Ecclaesiae christi Quæ est Bradfordæ per XL Annos Pastoris Vigilentissimi fui Commutavit Mortalem cum Immortali Die XXII Martii anno domini MDCCVII Aetatis Luci LXXI.

After the death of Mr. Symmes, the town having made trial of his ministerial endowments, voted to give a Mr. Stearns a call to settle with them, and for his support to give him 60 pounds for the first four years, and 65 the remainder of his life, the improvement of the parsonage, and thirty cords of wood. Why he did not accept is not mentioned. In July the 20th, 1708, the church voted to give Mr. Thomas Symmes, a son of their former minister, an invitation to settle with them, and the town voted the same day to concur with the church, and for his support to give him "both for quantity and quality" the same they had offered Mr. Stearns. He accepted the call and was installed December 1708, about a year after his father's death. Mr. T. Symmes was born in Bradford, February 1678, and was graduated at Harvard College, where he received his education in 1698. He was a man of strong powers of mind and of very considerable learning; often read in his family from the Hebrew Scriptures. He was the first minister in Boxford, ordained 1702, but was dismissed from them in 1708, the same year he was installed in this town. In early life his principles were not very strict, but he afterward embraced what are called the distinguishing doctrines of grace. He was a man of irritable if not of fiery passions, several instances are recollected in which his feelings got altogether the control of him, but he made it a uniform habit, as soon as the heat of the moment was over, to confess his sin, and if in his passion he had said any thing offensive to others, to ask their pardon. He wanted economy in the management of his pecuniary concerns, for with a better salary than any of his neighbours, he lived and died poor. He wanted prudence also in his intercourse with his people and in the measures he recommended and adopted for the common good. As evidence of this, I will mention a rule which he prevailed with the church to adopt, declaring it to be disorderly and a crime to be punished for church members to lean their heads down on their pews or rest them on their hands during public worship. And he laboured much with the parish to get them to pass a resolution to have the doors of the meeting-house closed the moment public worship commenced, and to suffer no one to come in after that. Though Mr. Symmes might go to extremes on these subjects, it must be felt that reformation is needed *here* and in most societies in these particulars, and I hope a hint of this kind will never again be called for to secure, in your practice, all which decency and order requires in this house of God. Mr. Symmes was a good singer himself, and was very resolute to introduce regular singing among his people, who were not at this time accustomed to such kind of singing, however contrary to their prejudices and inclinations. He wrote a kind of serio-jocose dialogue on the subject, which he published, and by these means raised a considerable party spirit in both places of his settlement. He was a man of very popular talents and made a figure in his profession. We may judge of his powers in the pulpit by what Rev. Mr. Coleman says of his election sermon preached 1720, "may it prove, says he, as profitable in the reading, as it was pleasant in the hearing, the preacher was unto us a very lovely song of one that has a pleasant voice, and can play well on an instrument." He was an uncommonly faithful man in all the parts of the gospel ministry, took special pleasure in giving instruction to the rising generation, published one sermon preached to the young men of his parish, which was much praised by Increase Mather, and which needs only to be read to be admired by all who have the things of religion at heart. He was very exact in self-examination, and spent much time in secret prayer, and was uncommonly anxious, and labored abundantly to have the church *without spot and blemish or any such thing*, and all its members walk in the faith. He was in favour of Congregational church government and greatly approved of that part of the Cambridge platform which recommends the having ruling elders in the church; and prevailed with his church to adopt that platform and to appoint elders. His ministry was attended with great success both in animating and quickening and edifying professors, and in awakening sinners, two or three considerable revivals took place during his ministry. In 1720, sixty-four were added to the church, forty-six of whom in three months, and twenty-five in one day, and there was but one year which passed without considerable accessions to the fold of Christ. Two hundred and seventy-three were received in the communion during his ministry. And on the 11th of June, two hundred and thirty-four persons united in commemorating their once crucified, but now risen Saviour, which number considering there were then but about two hundred families in town, I apprehend must have been very large even in those better days. Four hundred and seventy-four were baptized by him, and eighty-seven couples married. He died October 6th, 1725, aged 48, and the town voted fifty pounds to defray his funeral charges and continued for some time his salary to his widow. Besides those already mentioned, Mr. Symmes preached a sermon which he published. He also wrote and published an account of the fight at Pigwaket.*

*Upon his tomb stone is the following Inscription.*

Rev. Thomas Symmes died October the 6th, 1725, aged 48. He was an eminent christian, very lovely in his life, and every way an accomplished minister, of great industry, fidelity and concern for the generation after, saying, while I live I will seek their good, when I die write on my grave, here lies one who loved and sought the good of the rising generation.

In November following Mr. S. death, the town appointed Dea. Haseltine and Richard Bailey a committee to supply the pulpit, who engaged for this purpose Mr. Joseph Parsons, of Brookfield, to whom the church, after a time of trial, gave a call to settle with them in

* The memoirs of the life and ministry of Mr. Symmes, written by Rev. John Brown, formerly of Haverhill, is an extremely interesting little book. A new edition was published in 1816.

the work of the ministry, in which call the town concurred February 18th, 1726, and agreed to give him for his support, one hundred pounds salary, one hundred settlement, the parsonage and dwelling-house; and in April the same year, they added ten pounds more to his salary. Which offer he accepted and was ordained the 8th of June 1726. I have not been able to find any public account of his character and life. Those who knew him, speak of him as an amiable, pleasant man, a good public speaker, and as well liked by neighbouring societies. I should apprehend he was a man of less learning than his predecessors. His own people retained their attachment to him till his death, which took place on the 4th of May 1765, in the 63d year of his age, and 39th of his ministry. He was a very fine penman, and kept the church records with uncommon elegance and accuracy. During his ministry 288 were added to the church, 831 baptized, 176 married. In a memorandum attached to the church records, he observes, that the earthquake on the 29th October 1727, produced a great effect upon the minds of his people, and was the means of awakening their attention to things of religion. The same providence was followed with the same effect in this parish, and many were in consequence added to this church. Mr. Parsons preached the convention sermon in 1755, Math. v, 14, 15, 16.

*Upon his tomb stone is the following Inscription.*

This stone is placed over the dust of the Rev. Joseph Parsons, A. M. pastor of the first church in Bradford, as a testimony of the esteem and regard his flock bore to him, as an excellent minister and a christian, prepared for a better world. He was favoured with a quick and easy dismission from this, May 4th, 1765, in the 63d year of his age, and 39th of his ministry.

It was in June following the ordination of Mr. Parsons, that this parish was set off, which event was indeed, in contemplation, at the time Mr. Parsons received his call, and which induced the people of this part of town to vote against his settlement, not as they declared that they had ought against the man or doubted his ministerial qualifications, but because, contemplating a separation, they wished this to take place first, so as not to be involved in the expense of settling a man whose ministry they did not expect to enjoy.

Mr. Samuel Williams, of Waltham, succeeded Mr. Parsons in the west parish, he was ordained Nov. 20th 1765, and continued till January 14th, 1780, when he was dismissed in order to his accepting the professorship of Mathematicks and Natural Philosophy in Harvard University. He was, I suppose, a man of more learning, than any other whose ministry this town has enjoyed. He was known as a literary character, not only in this but in other countries, among whom he is spoken of with respect for his philosophical enquiries and observations. A circumstance took place at Cambridge which rendered his religious character questionable, but with the particulars of that unhappy transaction I am not acquainted. We should be careful not to form too decided an opinion of a man's character from a single fault. A gentleman who was well acquainted with him in Vermont, and who spent a considerable time in his family, informed me, he spent his time in useful studies, much esteemed for his great attainments, and for his sober and orderly life. His history of Vermont has passed through two editions, and is one of the best works of the kind, which have been written in this country. He died at Rutland, in 1817. During his ministry, the work of the Lord went on in that parish, 67 were added to the church, 225 baptized, and 85 married. He published while here, a sermon on repentance; also a Thanksgiving sermon, Psalm CXXXVII, 5, 6, entitled, love of our country.

Mr. Allen, the present minister followed him, and is

too well known by you to need any description of his character, and too much respected to need any praise from me. He was ordained June 8th, 1781; since which time there have been two considerable revivals, one in the year 1806, the other in 1812, which produced an observable change in the state of that people, as well as in the feelings and life of their venerable pastor. During his ministry, eighty-five have been added to the church, one hundred and eighty-one baptized, two hundred and one married. May God grant that he may still see the fruit of his labors, and many souls, among his people, gathered into the fold of Christ, before he sleeps with the generation of the dead. I have every reason to reverence and respect him for the very kind attention I have uniformly received from him since my settlement in this place.

This parish was, as we observed, set off and incorporated in June 1726, immediately upon which the people set about erecting a house for public worship, and placed it as you all know, but a little distance from the one in which we are now assembled. The first parish meeting was held the 4th of July 1726; Samuel Tenny was moderator. On the 8th of November this year, they voted unanimously to invite Mr. William Balch to preach with them, and on the 13th of March following, they gave him a call to settle with them, and for his support to give him one hundred pounds settlement, one hundred pounds salary, the improvement of the parsonage house and lot; and if at the end of four years Mr. Balch should signify under his own hand, that this was not enough for his comfortable support, they would add ten more, and if after experiment this was not found enough, they would add another ten pounds. Mr. Balch, after some alteration, mutually agreed on in the proposals, accepted the call and was ordained accordingly. I do not know that I can gratify your expectations better in regard to the character of Mr. Balch, and the circumstances of his ministry in this place, than to read to you the account given in Eliot's Biographical Dictionary, which is as follows:—

"William Balch, minister of the second church in Bradford, was born at Beverly in 1704. He possessed strong powers of mind; few of our New-England divines have surpassed him in clearness of perception, comprehension of understanding or soundness of judgment. The simplicity of his manners was peculiar, and he had a softness and benevolence in his disposition, which he discovered on occasions, where most men would have been irritated. He was graduated at Harvard College, 1724, ordained 1728, and died 1792, aged 88. The first years of his ministry were spent in peace and harmony with his people, and the neighbouring churches. At length a spirit of disorganization prevailed in many places, especially in the town near the Merrimack river. Nine members of Mr. Balch's church declared themselves dissatisfied with the preaching of their minister, and made a formal complaint to the brethren. The church thought the complaint unreasonable, and refused to act upon it. Hence the aggrieved party applied to a neighbouring church, to admonish their pastor and brethren, according to the direction of the platform, *by the third way of communion.* The church voted to call a council of the neighbouring churches, and the result was signed by the moderator, the venerable John Barnard, minister of the first church in Andover, blaming the conduct of those who complained, and approved the doings of the church. Mr. Balch published the whole proceedings in a quarto pamphlet, containing the letters that passed between him and the first church in Gloucester, and the transactions of both churches, till the dispute was settled. This was printed in 1744. Two years after the parochial difference, Messrs. Wigglesworth of Ipswich, and Chipman of Beverly, made a serious attack upon their brother for propagating Arminian tenets, and wrote an able defence of the doctrines of Calvin, which

were generally the sentiments of the New-England planters. It seems the former controversy began in 1644, by a
declaration of the aggrieved brethren, that "their pastor
propagated doctrines, not agreeing with the confession of
faith of these Congregational churches; and also, that the
church neglected the proper means of convicting said pastor of his errors." The gentleman who wrote against him
in 1746, had been assisting those who complained; and
they were not satisfied with the result of the council.
Their work, however, had no other effect than to draw
from Mr. B. a most able reply, in which he manifested a
temper that, with all his meekness, could feel rebuke.
There is[in it]much keen satire, mingled with sensible re-
marks and solid argument. The separatists in Bradford,
after this, built a meeting-house for themselves and the
disaffected members of other churches. Mr. Balch lived
to a good old age. His own flock esteemed and loved him,
and when he was advanced in years settled a colleague
He lived retired and was fond of husbandry, and the fruit
of his orchard was said to be the best in the county of Essex.
He was fond of the company of young men of talents, and
had fine colloquial powers, especially in discussing theo-
logical subjects. Being very desirous to read every thing
upon Ethics and Metaphysics, he made many enquiries
which discovered freedom of thought, and proved the en-
ergy of his mind did not fail him in those years, when our
strength is labour and sorrow.

P. S. His publications are, a discourse upon self-right-
eousness, in which he declares what are false confidences,
from the parable·of the Pharisee and Publican, 1742—
election sermon, 1749. His account of the proceedings
of the council and his reply to Messrs. W. & C. make two
pamphlets of more than fifty pages.

I have but little to add to this account of Mr. Balch. So
far as I am able to judge from the knowledge I have of
Mr. Balch, and the circumstances of his ministry here,
I am disposed to think the statement made in the above

extract, in regard to facts, is fair and correct, and will enable those of you who have only heard of these things, to form as correct an idea about this venerable man, and the circumstances of his ministry, as anything which could be said in the limits allowed to a discourse.

In regard to the sentiments which formed the subject of controversy between them, it will be of no importance for me to decide. All the parties have long since appeared before their judge. I should, however, think myself faulty, did I not suppose I had given you an opportunity of knowing my own views of these doctrines, for the correctness of which, I shall also have to give account.

So far as discipline was concerned, the simple question between the parties to be decided is, whether those of the church and neighbourhood, who were in sentiment Calvinistic, had a right, according to the then allowed organization of the church, to deal with Mr. Balch and other members of the church, who they thought were Arminian? And in the decision of this question it is to be presumed, there will be now, as there certainly was then, a diversity of sentiment. Before the death of Mr. Balch, several of his opponents became reconciled to him. One of them came to him and made formal and humble acknowledgment that he had wronged him, and from the character of Mr. Balch, we have no reason to question, but he heartily forgave him.

The last days of Mr. Balch, were calm and serene, and with the expression, "Come Lord Jesus, I am ready," he fell asleep.

It may not be uninteresting to know, that Mr. Balch was a descendant of Mr. John Balch, one of the first settlers in Beverly, who moved there from Dorchester, concerning whom Rev. Mr. White, one of the chief founders under God of the Massachusetts Colony, says, "he was an honest and good man." Beside the publications mentioned above, Mr. Balch published a sermon preached at the formation of the second church in Rowley, entitled "The duty of a christian church to manage their affairs with charity," 1 Cor. xvi. 14. And also a sermon preached before the convention of Congregational ministers.

*His tombstone has the following inscription.*

Erected to the memory of the Rev. William Balch, first pastor of the church in this place, who departed this life January the 12th, A. D. 1792, and in the 88th year of his age, and 64th of his ministry.

After Mr. Balch, through the infirmities of age become unable to discharge the duties of a pastor, an arrangement was made for settling a colleague, several candidates were employed, one of whom Mr. Chaplin from Rowley, now of Groton, received an invitation to setttle, and gave an answer in the affirmative. But as objections rose up before his ordination, a council was called and he was released. There was nothing however in these objections which bore unfavourably upon the ministerial character of Mr. Chaplin. The effect of this was, as might have been expected, the parish was divided into parties, and a great many persons were heard upon trial, before one was found in whom they could unite. But at length he who giveth pastors, through the instrumentality of the committee of supplies, brought Mr. Ebenezer Dutch to this place. His first sermon from the text, "buy the truth and sell it not," pleased all and united all. And in the beginning of the year 1779, both church and parish gave an unanimous vote for his settlement, with the exception of an individual, who said he voted against him to take off the curse pronounced against those of whom all speak well. A great abuse certainly of the real intention of that scripture. Mr. Dutch accepted the invitation, and was ordained November 17, 1779.

Mr. Dutch was born in Ipswich, was graduated at Providence College in 1776. So far as books are concerned, I suppose though respectable, he had less learning than any of his predecessors. He was a man however of an active, ready mind, possessed naturally great powers of speech, and when his feelings were particularly engaged, was as one certainly able to judge says, a man of "empassioned eloquence," and could without preparation hold forth on any subject connected with his profession, with great ease to himself and much to the satisfaction of his hearers. He was a man of quick feelings, and was in consequence often put off his guard. This produced excentricities, and contradictions, and irregularities in his conduct. And all will lament to say or think, that he engaged for a time too much in speculations of a worldly nature, a circumstance which proved injurious not only to his name but finally to his estate. But he that repenteth and forsaketh his sin shall find mercy. No one was more sensible of his mistake, sin if you will have it so, than Mr. Dutch himself finally became, and certainly no one more sorry for it. Most of you will recollect the sermon he preached from these words, "cut it down why cumbereth it the ground," after he became sensible of his errors, and also the acknowledgments he made on this occasion. His convictions were followed by amendment of life, for if in the middle part of his ministry the cares of this world occupied too much of his time, there was a most thorough reform, and no one could well be more diligent and faithful than he was the few last years of his life; and God be blessed he was permitted to see the fruits of his labour. Many in this place must acknowledge him as their father in Christ. His death as you all know, was very sudden, but the little time spared him, after he felt its approach, was spent in personal devotion, in words of exhortation, of comfort and reproof to those who came around him according as their particular circumstances seemed to require. He departed this life the 5th of August, 1813, aged 62, in the thirty-fourth year of his ministry. During his ministry there were 147 which were received to the church, 218 married. He did not keep an account of baptisms, a circumstance much to be regretted. He must have administered this ordinance to about three hundred. Mr. Dutch published two sermons, one preached at the dedication of this house, the other after the death of the first Mrs. Dutch.

*His tomb stone has the following Inscription.*

Rev. Ebenezer Dutch departed this life, August 4th, 1813, aged 62.

> As priests of old, so christian pastors die,
> But Christ the Lord, the great High Priest on high,
> And the good Shepherd, ever lives to save
> Those, for whose ransom, his own blood he gave,
> His church, he ever will defend and feed,
> And bring to endless life, a numerous seed,
> Those pastors, will a crown of glory wear,
> Who feed his lambs and sheep with faithful care.

Your present pastor was ordained the 28th of September, 1814. Since his coming among you, to January this year, there have been 33 added to the church, 47 infants and 12 adults baptized, 70 deaths, 200 births, and 34 marriages.

I should be considered guilty of an important omission did I not give some account of singing as it has been performed in our churches. A special attention to this lovely part of public worship was excited by the younger Symmes. Till his time the practice was to read one or two lines and then to sing them. A practice which prevailed universally in the early settlement of this country. He prevailed with the people to alter their practice in this respect, and was so happy by his exertions as to excite an attention, indeed to create a taste for this part of worship, which has in a degree continued to the present time. Perhaps few towns have been favored for a longer time with decent performance of this duty. In this parish, I do not know but in both since the division of the town, there has been a greater union of feeling and harmony of action, than is always found among those who join in this service. I have not learned of more than one considerable interruption of this good feeling in this parish since its incorporation. And this controversy was soon settled to the mutual and general satisfaction by some wise regulation adopted by the parish. There is now a large number of persons well acquainted with the rules of this science, and several who, if occasion called, could with great credit, take the lead in the choir. For this we are in a great measure indebted to the exertions and skill of the one who has, for many years, had the conduct of singing in this place. To whom this society is under great obligations for the part he has taken in this business, and I apprehend the public acknowledgment of this sentiment is nothing more than what is his just due.*

I should not however leave proper impressions of my ideas concerning the style of our music, did I not observe there is in it a degree of harshness, perhaps I ought to add noise, which very much diminishes the pleasure, if not the moral and religious effects which would otherwise be received from it. I know there are exertions now making to remedy this evil, and as all seem sensible of the need of reformation, I cannot but hope these exertions will be followed with the most perfect success.

Having thus called to your recollection some of the most important and interesting events connected with the history of this town, most of them, I know, important and interesting to none but ourselves, I shall conclude with a few observations which seem to arise from the subjects before us. And

1st. The people in this town have the greatest reason for gratitude for the good and pleasant land which the Lord their God has given them. Very few people are more favored in this respect than the people of this place. When they sow their seed it does really fall into that good ground which bringeth forth, some thirty, some sixty, and some a hundred fold. But it is not only those who get their riches from the increase of the field, who have reason to say their lines have fallen to them

* Captain Phineas Hardy.

in pleasant places, for such is the nature of business here, that all who are disposed may find full employment, and employments suited to their capacities whether in the dawn of life, or arrived to the strength and vigour of manhood, or sinking under the infirmities of age. There may be places where large possessions can be more readily acquired, but I question whether there is one in this commonwealth, where means of comfortable living can be more easily obtained, or indeed where they are more generally enjoyed. And it would be easy by the mention of individuals, to support the declaration, that here also the hand of the diligent maketh rich. If these things are so, and I appeal to all sober minded and considerate persons for the truth of them, I would ask whether, except in instances of real misfortunes, those who are destitute of things necessary and convenient, have not great reason to look for the real cause, in some fault or folly of their own.

2d. From the care this town has taken to select out and appoint to office men of good report, those who looked not only to their own things, but also to the things of others, the public concerns of this town have been wisely and prudently conducted; very few instances occur, from the earliest settlement to the present time, of any considerable default in any of the officers in the town. And in consequence of the measures the town has at different times adopted to preserve order in their assemblies, the meetings for the transaction of town and parish business, have generally been decent and orderly, thus affording all present an opportunity to see and hear what was doing and of acting understandingly, in the parts they took in the various business brought before them. And though in the various transactions of the town for 170 years, there must have been in many instances a diversity of sentiment and judgment, yet upon the whole there is upon the records great evidence of a general disposition to think and act together.

3d.  From what the town has done to furnish instruction to the rising generation.  A knowledge competent to the conduct of the common concerns of life, has been acquired by most who have lived in this town, and there have always been a competent number of well instructed persons, able to transact all the business of the town in a correct and orderly way.  The public records have been well kept, and I should be guilty of an omission did I not observe this has been particularly the case since they have been in the hands of the present clerk, who has served the town in this office about twenty years.*  And though there have not risen many men, strictly called great, yet there have been those respectable in the councils of the State, and distinguished on the battle ground.  There have also been and still are in the several professions, men whom the town calls her sons, with whose standing in life she has much reason to be satisfied.

4th.  From the part the town, in common with others, took in the great enterprise which gave independence to these United States, you enjoy a free government, equal laws, and a mild administration; your personal, civil and religious rights are all secured to you; your *nobles are of yourself, and your governours proceed from the midst of you.*  There is indeed no other nation upon the globe, where the people are so free and happy, where the means of comfortable, I may say genteel subsistence, can be so generally acquired, or where every one has so full and unrestrained an opportunity of directing his talents and labors in the way and to the purposes most agreeable to himself.

5th.  In consequence of the exertions which the people of this town have made, to enjoy in a decent and comfortable way, the ordinances of religion, they have been furnished with convenient places for holding their religious assemblies.  Six houses have been erected for this

* William Greenough, Esq.

purpose, two by the town, while they worshipped together, one by the west parish, two by this parish, and one by those who separated from this because of their disaffection to Mr. Balch. Three of these like those who worshipped in them, have fallen under the weight of years. Two of them are now standing in this town, and afford convenience to those who are disposed to worship God in company, and so prepare for a better country, where the righteous will find a building not made with hands, eternal and in the heavens, large enough for the whole congregation of the just.

6. The people have not only had houses for public worship, they have had ministers of the Lord also, to lead in the services of these sanctuaries. Very few years I believe, hardly seven in the whole, since 1668, have passed, but the people have beheld their teacher. And even during the short intervals which have passed, between the removal of one and the settlement of another pastor, the pulpits have been so supplied, that for 170 years, hardly a sabbath has passed, but the word of God has been read and explained in the public congregations of the people, and I shall be supported by all who have knowledge on the subject, when I say for the most part, by those who were able to teach and willing to wait on the things of the ministry. If there is any advantage then in the constant enjoyment of an able and faithful ministry, this town has had it as fully, I presume, as any other town in the Commonwealth. What improvement individuals have made of the price thus put into their hands to get wisdom, must be left to the decision of the great day. That there are real and substantial benefits connected with the ministry of the word and ordinances, is as certain as the word of God and the history of the church can make it. Both the word of God and the history of ages, teach us that, *faith cometh by hearing,* and that *by the foolishness of preaching* it pleases God *to save those that are lost.* The

records of our churches bear evidence, that this ordinance of the Lord has not been in vain in this place. For previous to the separation of the town into parishes, there were 399 gathered into the visible church; since that time 333 have been added to the church in the west parish, 542 to that in this, making 1284 in all. While the town worshipped together there were 837 baptized, since that 1175 have been served with this ordinance in the west parish; and if our calculations concerning the number baptized by Mr. Dutch be correct, something more than a 1000 in this, making together more than 3000. Of those who have made profession of religion, about 1100 had received the ordinances of baptism in infancy, the remainder, amounting to about 184, were baptized upon profession. And now, in review of these facts let us, with the full impression of the immense value of souls upon our minds, ask ourselves whether the hopeful piety of 1284 persons, who actually professed religion together with those who may have obtained a saving interest in Christ, but did not, from various causes, unite outwardly with his visible kindom, and also the baptism of nearly half of all who have lived and died in this place, is not more than a hundred fold reward for all the expense the town has been at, to support the worship and ordinances of God. Or even, if you suppose many may have professed the name of Christ, who notwithstanding had not received him into their hearts, would not those who remain after all the deductions that you can think ought to be made, be a more than full return for all that has been done in this place, to promote the salvation of souls.

7. And to the question, *What profit is there in baptism?* do not the records of our churches reply as an apostle did in relation to another ordinance, whose real design bore a striking resemblance to this? *Much every way.* About one third of all, who have in this town been served in early life with this ordinance, have in mature age

made a profession of faith in Christ in some of our
churches. It is known also that many, who received this
ordinance in this place, have professed Christ in other
towns to which they had in the providence of God removed. Above three hundred are still living, concerning whom both the promises of God and the past history
of our churches, justify us in the hope that many of them
will, at some time, do better things than to continue in unbelief. While from among a greater number who had
not this seal of the covenant put upon them, something
short of two hundred have in after life confessed Christ
before men. I make these observations in relation to
facts connected with the history of redeeming love in
this place—facts too, which call for the serious consid-
eration of all who make the things of religion the subject of their concern; bearing in my own breast, at the
same time feelings of good will towards those who differ
from me, in regard to the requirement of God respecting
the proper subject of this ordinance. And I hope I shall
be believed when I say, it is my earnest prayer that all
in this place, who love the Lord Jesus Christ, may
really love one another, and so doing we shall have
reason to hope, if in anything we be differently minded,
*God will in due time reveal even this unto us.*

8. But when we have the greatest reason to thank
God because so much good has resulted from the enjoyment of his ordinances in this town, we have also reason
for the deepest regret that so many have apparently
neglected this salvation. The whole number who have
lived and died or do still live in this town, according to the
best counting I can make, is about 7000, of whom, as we
have already mentioned, 1284 have made open profession of having obtained a saving interest in the Lord
Jesus Christ. If we should reduce this number, by taking from it all, who may have been suspected of having
a name to live, while they were really dead, and compare
what are left with those who made no pretentions to re-

ligion, and those the world judged to have none, what a striking illustration shall we have of the words of the Saviour, *That wide is the gate and broad is the way that leadeth to destruction and many there be that go in thereat; while strait is the gate and narrow is the way that leadeth unto life and few there be that find it.* A number may be considerable in itself, and yet comparatively small, and such is the case in relation to those who have in this town professed an interest in Christ; 1284 persons gathered into his visible kingdom, and in charitable hope saved from wrath through him, is such a display of divine goodness and such an overflowing return for all that has been done here to promote his cause, we can never sufficiently adore His unspeakable grace, whose Spirit has done all this. And yet how lamentable to reflect, a number five fold greater have neglected the offers of salvation. Does it not, my friends, seem strange that so many, who lived before you, with all the advantages they enjoyed for acquainting themselves with God so as to be at peace with him; advantages too, which others improved to their salvation, should notwithstanding continue impenitent and unbelieving; and is it not equally strange that you, who are this day without faith, should walk in the same way of unbelief. Your advantages for attending to the concerns of your souls are great, and your opportunities for religious instruction numerous; what reasons then have you for thus neglecting the offers of recovering mercy and pardoning grace? Or what is there in your case, which in the place of torment will prove any such alleviation to your sufferings as to justify you in the present neglect of this great salvation. The space afforded you to make your peace with God is passing swiftly away. Consider the former generations. *Our fathers where are they?* Four generations since the settlement of this town all sleep the sleep of death. Of the fifth but here and there one remains to tell us of the years that are past, while those of the sixth pass for old men and old women among us.  *And the prophets, do they live for ever?*  Six, who have ministered here in holy things, have been gathered to the fathers, all but one of whom slumber in the same ground with those who received instruction from their lips.  These all rest from their labours, and their works have followed them.  And you, my friends, will soon sleep in the same dust.  Give all diligence then to make your calling and election sure.  For though they sleep, though the earth has received them out of our sight, and the grave has closed upon them, the Lord hath his eye upon them, counts their numbers, weighs all their dust in a balance, writes all their members in his book; not a part will be lost, not an individual will be overlooked, not one be left unrecovered from the ground;—they will all rise and come forth out of their graves, and you will rise also and come forth out of your graves, and we shall all meet at the judgment seat of Christ.  At that time and at that place, you will meet with all, whose names have been called to recollection this day, and all, who have lived in this town, and indeed with all, who have lived in all other towns, states and kingdoms.  What a solemn and interesting day!  The Judge of quick and dead will then be upon his seat, the books open, the trumpet sounding, the universe assembling.  Towns and parishes, their pastors as their leaders, in company approaching the final tribunal; heaven and hell, the everlasting dwellings of the righteous and the wicked, in view, and nothing remaining but the awful sentence to be pronounced, and the condition of all is fixed for ever————

> "A point of time, a moment's space,
> Removes us to yon heavenly place,
> Or——locks us up in hell."

My friends, is it not prudent to prepare beforehand for this solemn, interesting day; and, since all your actions are written in the book of the chronicles kept in heaven, to see that your names are also recorded in the book of life.

Now unto Him that is able to keep you from falling and to present you faultless before the presence of His glory with exceeding joy, to the only wise God our Saviour be glory and majesty, dominion and power both now and for ever.—AMEN.

## ERRATA.

Page 8, 7th line from the top, for 1700, read 1750
Page 15, 3d line from the top, for *have been given orders*, read *orders have been given.*
Page 53, 2d line from the top, for *to January this year*, read *in January that year.*

# APPENDIX,

Containing a number of interesting facts, some omitted by mistake in copying the discourse for the press, others of such a nature, as could not well be introduced into the body of the discourse, and a few not known at the time.

1. The first person born in Rowley, on record, was Edward Carlton, born 1639, ancestor of those of that name in this town. The other persons born this year, were Thomas Migall, ancestor of the first Mrs. Dutch, Jonathan Lambert, Jonathan Remmington, and Mary Jackson. William Tenny, the great grandfather of our Deacon Tenny, was born 1640, and was chosen Deacon in 1667 ; and it is a circumstance worthy of notice, that there have been in our churches of his descendants, persons bearing that office, from that time to the present day ; and several of the same family have held the same office in other churches. In October, 1639, Robert and Anna Haseltine were married ; the first couple on record. November 14, 1682, Anah widow of Robert Haseltine and Anah widow of Thomas Hardy, were received into the church in this town ; and were as a note attached to the church records by Mr. Symmes, informs us, the first received by confession. The first birth recorded in this town, is that of Martha Wilford, daughter of Gilbert Wilford, born January 18th, 1671. The first death recorded, is that of John Simmonds, son of John Simmonds, July 20th, 1671. The first marriage, is that of William Hardy and Ruth Tenny, May 3d, 1678. The first person baptized, was Hannah, daughter of John and Hannah Boynton, December 11th, 1682.

2. The following persons have held the office of Deacon in this town.

*Time of appointment.* *Names.*                     *Deceased.*            *Age.*

| | David Haseltine, | |
|---|---|---|
| |     Woodman, | |
| 1712 | Richard Bailey, | *While the town worshipped together.* |
| 1712 | Samuel Tenny, | |
| 1718 |     Hall. | |

### IN THE WEST PARISH.

| | | |
|---|---|---|
| 1728 | Moses Day, | |
| 1730 | Joseph Hall, | |
| 1730 | Thomas Kimball, | |
| | Thomas Carlton, | |
| 1745 | David Walker, | |
| 1750 | Moses Day, | |
| 1754 | Stephen Kimball, | |
| 1762 | Obediah Kimball, | |
| 1797 | Richard Walker, | |
| 1804 | John Griffin, | |
| 1806 | John Hasseltine, | |

### IN THE EAST PARISH.

| | | | |
|---|---|---|---|
| 1727 | Richard Bailey, | | |
| 1728 | William Hardy, | died 1747. | aged 81 |
| 1747 | Jonathan Tenny, | | |
| 1759 | Nathaniel Jewett, | removed to Hollis. | |
| 1764 | Timothy Hardy, | Obt. 1777, small pox. | |
| 1764 | Phillip Tenny, | Obt. 1783. | aged 77 |
| 1777 | William Balch, | | |
| 1779 | Thomas Tenny, | | |
| | Phineas Carlton, | | |
| 1797 | William Tenny, | | |
| 1804 | Daniel Stickney, | | |
| 1806 | Thomas Morse. | | |

It is apprehended this is considerably short of a full catalogue of those who have held the office of Deacon in this town, particularly of those who were in office before the town was divided into parishes. Such is the writing of the first Mr. Symmes, I have not been able yet to decypher but a part of the records made by him, and since his day there must have been a deficiency in recording the names of those called to the office of Deacon, as I have found from enquiry, the names of some who are not upon record, or I have been so unfortunate, after repeated search, as not to notice them.  In the conclusion of this article, it becomes my pleasing duty to remark, that, from all the enquiry that I have made, and from the evidence afforded by the records of the church, there is the greatest reason to believe, that most or all who have been appointed to this office, have been *men of honest report, full of the Holy Ghost and wisdom*, who *used the office of a Deacon well.*

March the 18th, 1718, Richard Bailey and Samuel Tenny, were, agreeably to the recommendation of the Cambridge platform, appointed to the office of ruling Elders.  Of the former of these I have no particular knowledge, farther than what may safely be inferred from a declaration which Mr. T. Symmes has left on record, as what he himself said to the church when assembled to appoint persons to this office ; that he "would be content if they would appoint the two aged deacons to the office of Elders," of whom Mr. Bailey was one. Of Elder Tenny, who was the other, and who upon the division of the town into parishes, was appointed to the same office in this church, it would be easy to write a considerable of a volume, filled with interesting circumstances. He was, I apprehend, both by nature and grace, one of the most distinguished men this town and ever produced ; and as he grew old, was truly patriarchal.  The old people, now living, who knew him in some of his last years, recollect with pleasure and thankfulness, the good instruction he gave them in early life. He could write in short hand, and was in the habit of taking off the sermons he heard, and used to spend the intermission on sabbath days, in reading these over to the people who stayed at the meeting-house, in praying with them, and in communicating to them good and wholesome instruction. As he deserved, so he received the respect and confidence of the town, being in most of its concerns, preferred to those offices which were considered the most respectable or involved the greatest trust. One anecdote I shall record not because it is the most interesting that might be presented, but because it may be instrumental in calling the attention of some, especially of the rising generation, to a circumstance which perhaps they do not sufficiently think of. The old gentleman had a plum tree standing by the road a little out of sight from the house which on a certain year, bore pretty fully ; about the time these were ripe, a young man of the neighborhood passing by and thinking no one was in sight, gave the tree a shake and then with great haste went to picking up the plums which fell to the ground. At this moment the old gentleman providentially came out. But before he had said any thing, the young man under all the embarrassment of the moment, began to make his excuse and plead as an apology for what he was doing, that he had shaken the tree but *once*. To which the old gentleman made this simple reply, that if every one should do the same, that he himself should not be able to shake even *once*. This reply, while it suggests an interesting truth, is said to have had a most salutary effect upon the youth. And I hope that its repetition here may serve, as one inducement among others, to prevent the rising generation from exposing themselves to the chagrin which this transgressor must have experienced. Elder Tenny's house was just below Mr. Nathaniel Wallingfords.

3. The town's expense in 1720, was 60*l*. 16*s*. 4*d*. in 1820, 900*l*. average for the ten years past, 2700 dollars. From which circumstance may be known, in some degree, the increase of wealth in this place, for the last hundred years. It does not appear that the tax now is

greater according to the value of property than it was then.

The average expense for maintaining the poor, the last 10 years, has been 839 dollars.†

The following circumstance will give some idea of the increase in the value of land. Before Thomas Kimball moved into this town, probably about the year 1660 or a little after, he was driving a herd of cattle through on his way to Haverhill or Hampstead, when he was met by one of the land holders in this place, probably Haseltine, who offered to take his cattle at a generous price, and to let him have land upon the river at eight pence an acre in exchange.

4. *First Settlers.*—This town was at first laid out in lots, running from the river to what is now called the Rowley line. These lots were of different widths, but the boundaries of most of them are easily discoverable by the course of the fences. And a sufficient number of them are still in the possession of the descendants of the first inhabitants, to give any one much acquainted in town, an idea sufficiently accurate of the place where the first people lived, and the land they occupied. We will repeat their names in order, beginning at the east end of the town. These were Joseph Richardson, Jonas Platts, John Hopkinson, Joseph Bailey, Edward Wood, * Benjamin Savory, William Hutchens, * Ezra Rolf, Samuel Tenney, Frances Jewett, Samuel Wooster. His lot was the one on which Mr. William Balch now lives. Next to this was that of Samuel Stickney. Then followed that of *John and *William Hardy, brothers ; who it is said came into this country in the family of Gov. Winthrop as labourers. But he, not finding business for them, gave them at first land at Ipswich, but as they

† Since the writing of this discourse, the town has purchased a house and farm for the use of the poor, where it is presumed they will be made more comfortable, and the expense of maintaining be less than formerly.

did not like the soil, he gave them leave to come to this town, and furnished them with their patent. Their house stood just back of Mr. David Mardin's, where the cellar may now be seen. Next to them was the Phillips Patent, settled by Abraham and Daniel Parker, cousins; the former born in Rowley, the other from Chelmsford. Their house stood almost in the same place that Stephen Parker's well now occupies. Next to them was the Carleton patent. They lived near the Mills described before. Then was the Haseltine Patent extending from near the mouth of Johnson's Creek to Chadwick's Ferry, and was settled by Thomas Kimball, whose place of residence we have already described, *William Jackson, *David Hazeltine, Shubel Walker, *Abraham Haseltine and Capt.      Woodman. Then followed the lots of Thomas West, whose house stood near where Abijah Gage now lives, and that of John Boynton and John Griffin. Next to them and extending to Andover line, was the patent of John Day, whose house was the fourth built in the West Parish. On his lot were three original settlers, beside himself, * Nehemiah Carlton, * Richard Hale and * Alexander Campbell. The land on the Neck, so called, was patented to * Philip Atwood and John Head.. Abraham Gage, John Annis and Samuel Kimball settled with them.


5. The following are the names of Physicians, who have resided in this place. It is not known that they stand in the order of life.      Bailey, John Bishop, from Ireland, Ezekiel Chace, Benjamin Muzzy, John Tenny, who died with the small pox, Seth Jewett, Elijah Proctor, Manley Hardy, Ebenezer Jewett died in 1817, and Dr. Benjamin Parker and Jeremiah Spofford, the present practioners.

*Note.* It is not absolutely certain though highly probable that the christian names having this mark * are correct.

6. There is a Post-office in this town opened in 1811, and was granted at the instance of Benjamin Parker, Esq. Such are the arrangements at present in this office, that the people in both Parishes are almost as well accommodated as though there was one in both places.

7. In addition to the mechanics already enumerated, we ought to mention, that the town is well furnished with well-taught carpenters, blacksmiths, masons and painters. And indeed with tradesmen of almost every description, whose personal services are needed in common life, and it is with real satisfaction, that I add, that the most of them are men of industrious habits and sober lives.

8. Peat, and of a very good quality, abounds in this town. Large and increasing quantities of it are cut every year. And such is the extent of the meadows, that there is the fullest reason to believe, people of many generations will be supplied with good fuel without any considerable advance from the present price. It is moreover the opinion of good judges on the subject, that the quantity of wood has not diminished but rather increased for the 30 years past. And a few, among whom is Mr. Daniel Spofford, have commenced the cultivation of wood, by sowing, on suitable land, acorns, walnuts, &c., an example, which it will undoubtedly be wise for those to follow who have rough and waste land.

The soil in this town is, as has been observed, generally good; it is also much benefitted by the large quantities of salt hay, which are yearly brought into town; but its produce might still be greatly increased by the proper use of Plaster of Paris. And it is not a little surprising, after what is known on the subject, that this article is so little used in this town and vicinity. I have found it of the greatest service in my garden. It is well known that Mr. David How, of Haverhill, who so far as the cultivation of land is concerned, is not only one of the greatest but best farmers in this part of the county, makes great use of and finds it of great service. And why should it not be equally beneficial to others, and if so why not use it?

9. *Meeting Houses.* When the first meeting-house was built I have not been able to ascertain. It must have been, as appears from circumstances, several years before the first meeting of the town on record. In 1705 a vote passed to build a new meeting house, 48 feet long and 42 broad; but it was afterwards voted it should be 40 feet wide and 20 feet between plate and sill; and Capt. David Haseltine, John Chadwick and Ensign Joseph Bailey were appointed a committee to inquire about the expense of such a building, and Capt. Haseltine, Cornet Richard Kimball, and John Hutchins a committee to carry on the building.

In 1726, the year the town was divided into parishes, this parish built their first meeting-house. Standing as you all know, but a little distance from the one in which we now worship.

In 1790 the one in which we now worship was built. The committee entrusted with the direction of this were Bradstreet Parker, Phineas Carlton, William Balch, Samuel Adams, Retier H. Parker, Thomas Morse and Peter Russell. The contractors were Phineas Carleton, Ebenezer Hopkinson, Silas Hopkinson, Edward Sargent; and the sum for which they undertook it was £6.2 8 0; and it is no more than justice to say, the plan does great credit to the committee who contrived it, and the work to those who performed it. It is certainly a very convenient and neatly finished house. I wish I could add, that it was in all respects in that state of perfect repair which a true regard to beauty and economy really requires.

About the year 1750 those who separated from this Parish bought a meeting-house in Rowley, and moved it into the east part of the town, where they met, for some time, for religious services. This building has since been removed, and is now improved by the Baptist society in Rowley.

The west parish built their present meeting-house in 1751. The committee appointed to attend to the building of this were Benjamin Gage, Daniel Thurston, Nathaniel Gage, Josiah Chandler and Moses Gage.

10. It was observed in the discourse, that this town was always ready and did in reality bear its full proportion of the expense and labour of the revolutionary war. One instance of the remarkable preservation of the lives of those, from this town, in the day of battle, is worthy of being recorded. Capt. Nathaniel Gage, with a company of 40 men from this town was in the Battle at Bunker Hill, and in a place much exposed to the enemy, an yet not a life was lost. This company had been instructed in military manœuvres by an English deserter who is still living in H——. And was one of the best disciplined and most effective companies engaged in that ever-memorable day.

There was something of a similar preserving providence extended to the company, which marched from this to Stillwater, N. Y. during the French war of 1755, under the command of Capt. William Kimball. All of whom returned again to their own homes in safety. The journal of Capt. K. during his service has been preserved and is now in the hands of Jesse Kimball, Esq.

11. There are in the East parish 121 houses; 165 families; 131 married couples; 10 widowers; 36 widows; 39 male and 71 female members of the Congregational church now in the parish. The whole number belonging to the church about 130. 9 Calvinistic Baptist pro-

fessors ; 9 Free-will Baptist professors ; 170 baptized persons not in full communion. About 500 persons under 21 ; 10 above 80 ; and 850 in all. In the West parish there are 94 houses ; 97 married couples ; 8 widowers ; 24 widows ; 25 male and 35 female members of the Congregational church ; 12 Calvinistic Baptist professors ; 15 Free-will Baptist professors ; about 450 under 21 years ; 8 above 80 ; 800 in all.

And now before I come to a final conclusion, I will take this opportunity to express my obligations to all, who have assisted me in collecting any of the facts contained in this discourse, particularly to the old, for the cheerfulness with which they have heard and answered my many inquiries. And I will further observe, however highly I may have esteemed and respected them before, I have, from the intercourse, which the writing of this discourse has caused me to have with them, found abundant cause still more highly to esteem and respect them, especially when in addition to the wisdom which experience has taught them, their old age *is found in the ways of righteousness*. And I do believe, did the youth know what a fund of useful information they have, information too, which can be found only with them, concerning the ways of God and the conduct of men in this town, and the interesting manner, in which many of them communicate this knowledge, their company would be sought for as that from which the greatest delight and pleasure were to be derived.